Gus

Olivier Dunrea

HOUGHTON MIFFLIN HARCOURT
Boston   New York

To access the read-along audio file, visit
WWW.HMHBOOKS.COM/FREEDOWNLOADS
ACCESS CODE: WATCH

AGES	GRADES	GUIDED READING LEVEL	READING RECOVERY LEVEL	LEXILE® LEVEL
4-6	1	F	9-10	480L

The text was set in Shannon. The illustrations are pen-and-ink and gouache on 140-pound d'Arches coldpress watercolor paper.

The Library of Congress Cataloging-in-Publication Data is on file.

ISBN: 978-0-544-93723-9 paper-over-board
ISBN: 978-0-544-93724-6 paperback

Manufactured in China
SCP 10 9 8 7 6 5 4 3 2 1
4500635250

For Ed, still quiet and observent as ever

This is Gus.

Gus is a small yellow gosling
who likes to be by himself.

Gus sits in a haystack, watching
a tiny red spider spin a web.

Gus stands on a wooden box
in the barn.

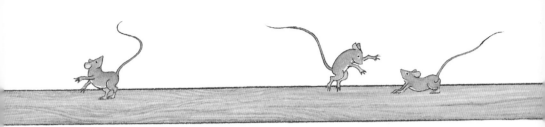

He watches the mice scamper
along the beam.

Gus waddles to the pond.
He pokes his head underwater.

Gus quietly watches the turtle
scraping in the dirt.

Gus watches the turtle
slowly slip into the water.

Gus scoots to the hole where
the turtle was digging.

Gus peers down the hole.

He gently pokes in the dirt.

He sees three small eggs.

Gus carefully sits on the eggs.

He watches the barn mice
scurry past.

He watches the raindrops.

He drowsily watches a snail
sneak by in the moonlight.

Gus quietly sits and watches.

Suddenly Gus feels the
eggs move!

Gus hops off the eggs.

He watches the eggs
split open!

Three small green heads
peek out of the shells.

Gus stares at the tiny turtles.

The baby turtles stare at Gus.

Gus is a small yellow gosling
who likes to be by himself.
Most of the time.

DATE DUE